LOOK & LEARN™

How A Hospital Works

Alex Woolf

BOOK HOUSE
a SALARIYA imprint

Contents

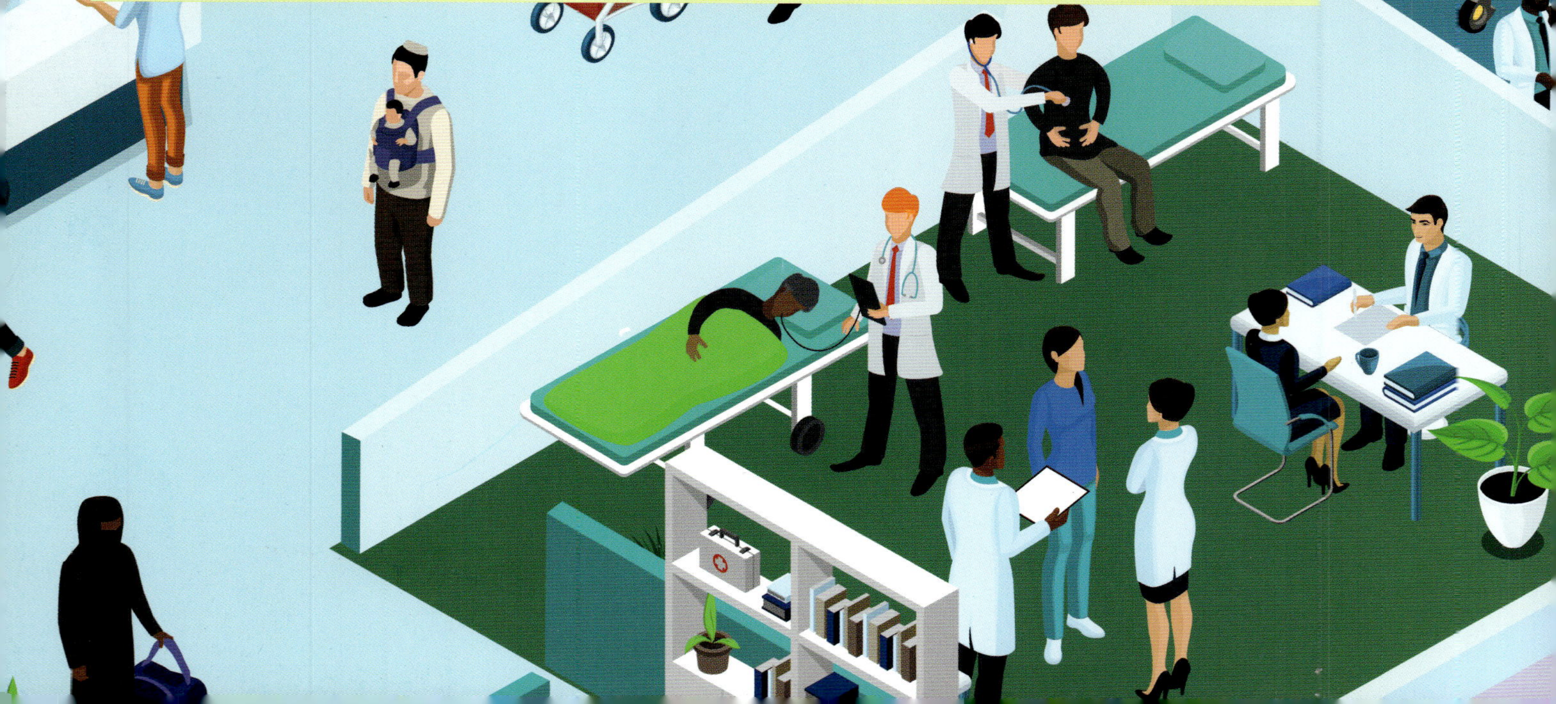

Introduction

Hospitals are places where people receive medical treatment and care. The staff include doctors, nurses, administrators and a wide range of support staff. Hospitals are divided up into different departments, or wards. Accident and Emergency deals with patients requiring urgent medical treatment of any kind. Other wards specialise in different fields of medicine. Catering for patients with many different needs makes hospitals busy, complex places. Therefore it is essential that they are well-designed and administered so they can run efficiently. In this book we look at how hospitals work, who runs them, what they do and how they function.

Who runs hospitals?

The needs of all staff and patients, including their food, safety and a healthy environment, must be looked after. To run efficiently, a hospital needs good financial management, IT and communications, record keeping, staff recruitment, quality control and effective marketing. The medical staff (the doctors and nurses) can then do their job efficiently. A hospital therefore requires a team of administrators to run it.

Hospital administrator

A hospital administrator is in overall charge, ensuring that everything runs smoothly for staff and patients. The long-term future of the hospital must be considered and decisions made about any investments in major equipment or IT systems. They also ensure the hospital complies with government laws and regulations.

Finance

The hospital administrator sets the budget, and the hospital's finance department will spend the money where it's needed, and within budget.

Human resources

The human resources department recruits and dismisses hospital staff, keeps up to date with the laws on employment, and keeps staff records. They also oversee holiday and sick leave.

You are here

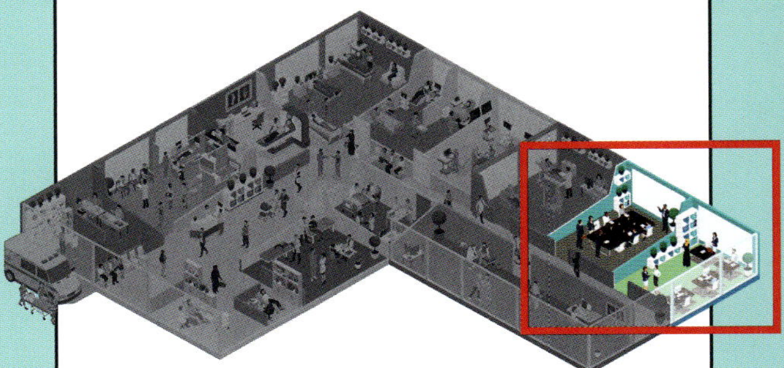

S.T.E.A.M solutions

Modern hospitals use computers linked up to an IT system in order to function efficiently. The system, carrying the health information and full history of all patients, is accessible by staff in every ward. This saves time and also reduces costs. Instead of gathering information from patients at every stage, doctors can spend more time treating them.

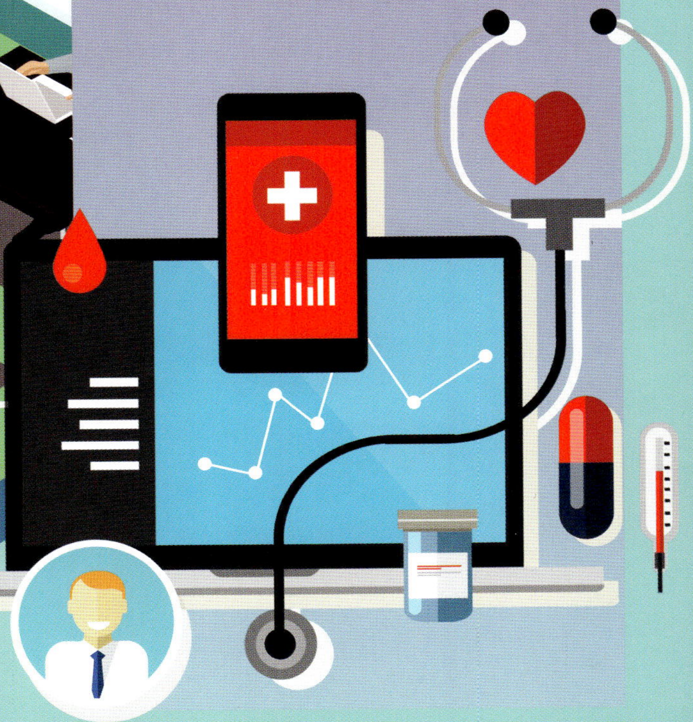

How do hospitals deal with emergencies?

Victims of an accident or sudden, serious illness are taken to a hospital's Accident and Emergency ward (A&E). Patients can arrive at any time, and staff must deal with all kinds of medical emergencies with little or no warning. It's a high-pressure environment where life-and-death decisions have to be made very quickly. Most A&E wards are located on the hospital's ground floor and have their own entrance to allow for easy access. Patients are treated according to the urgency of their case.

Triage

Many large A&Es have staff who perform triage – the prioritising of patients according to need. Minor problems are treated by a doctor in A&E. More serious cases are transferred to the relevant hospital ward to see specialist doctors and nurses.

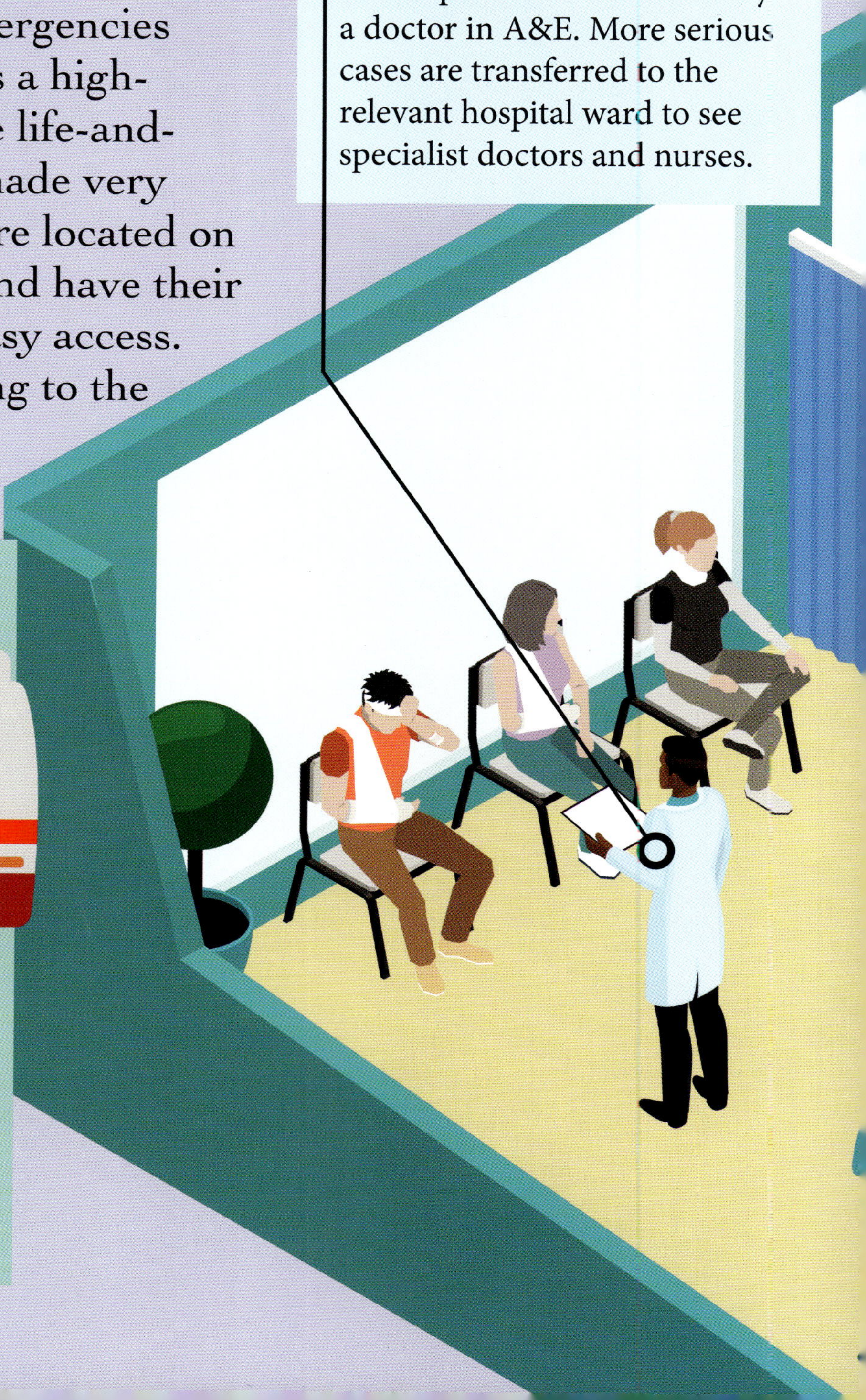

Ambulance

Paramedics on board an ambulance can administer emergency care en-route. Ambulances have lights and sirens to cut quickly through traffic.

Trauma

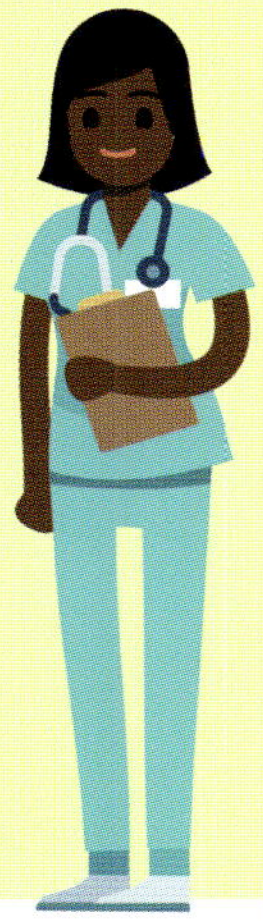

Many hospitals have a 'trauma' centre. This is like an A&E, but it specialises in dealing with major injuries, such as falls, road collisions, burns or gunshot wounds. Surgeons and nursing staff who are trained in life support work there.

You are here

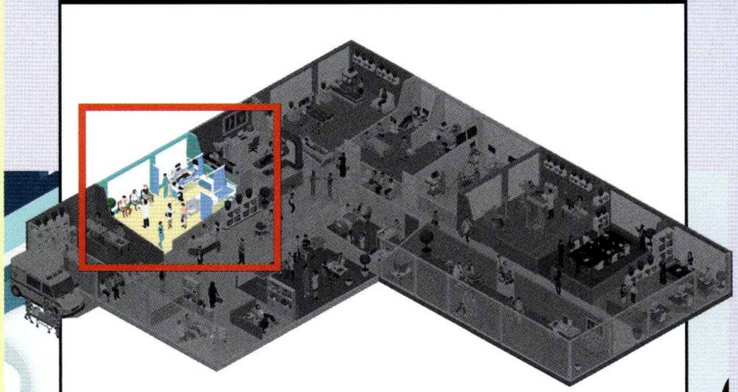

S.T.E.A.M solutions

In A&E wards, technology plays an important role in both diagnosis and life support. Radiography (the use of X-rays to see inside the body) is used to assess the severity of injuries. Computed tomography (CT) scans can show bone fractures, tissue damage and ruptured organs. Hospitals are also equipped with defibrillators, which provide an electric current to a patient's heart to start it beating again.

Defibrillator

How are seriously ill patients cared for?

The intensive care unit (ICU) is a ward that provides treatment and monitoring for patients who are very ill. Patients in ICU may have recently had major surgery, they may have problems with one or more organs, or be unable to eat or breathe on their own. In hospitals with no trauma centre, patients with severe wounds are also treated in ICU. When they no longer need intensive care, patients are transferred to another ward before eventually going home.

Pain relief

Medical conditions and some treatments can cause physical discomfort and mental distress. Patients are given drugs for pain relief along with sedatives to make them sleepy.

Monitoring

Patients in ICU require round-the-clock observation. They are cared for by specialist nurses who are normally assigned to look after just one or two patients. Machines constantly monitor the patients' health conditions.

You are here

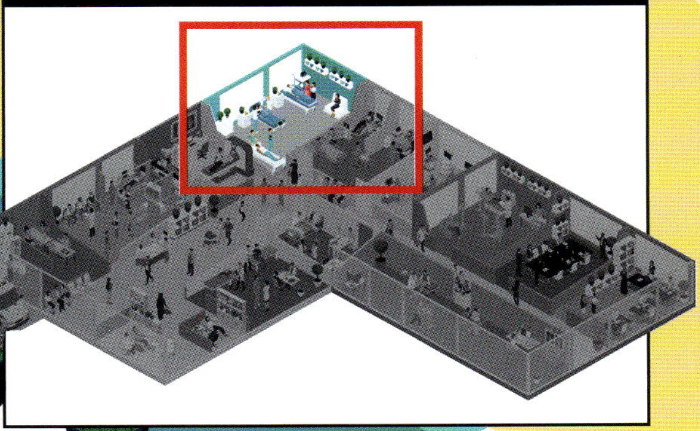

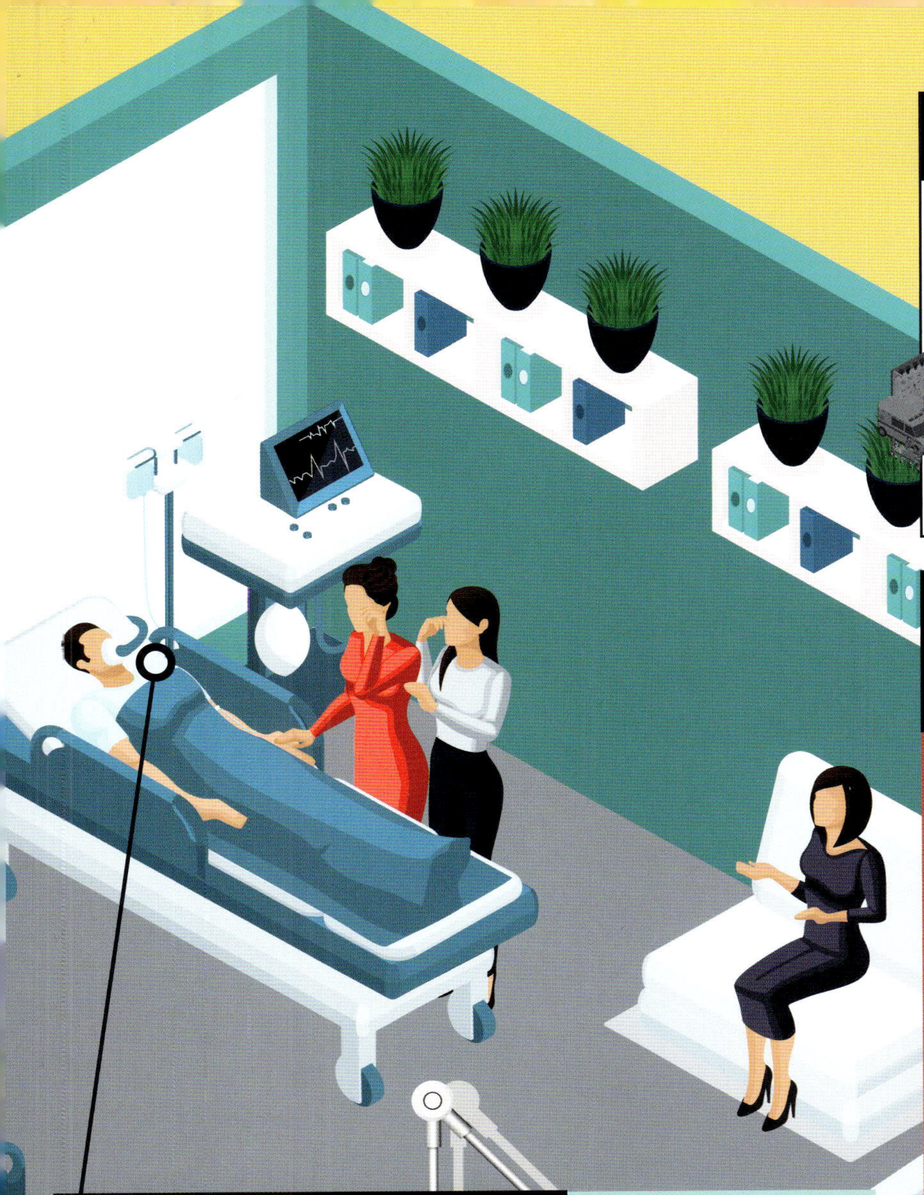

S.T.E.A.M solutions

Technology is used in ICU wards to monitor a patient's pulse rate, temperature, breathing rate, blood pressure and level of oxygen in the blood. Sensors attached to the patient constantly measure these vital signs to send this data to a device called a hospital monitor. It converts the signals from the sensors into a format that can be shown on a screen. Warning sounds alert medical staff to abnormalities in the vital signs.

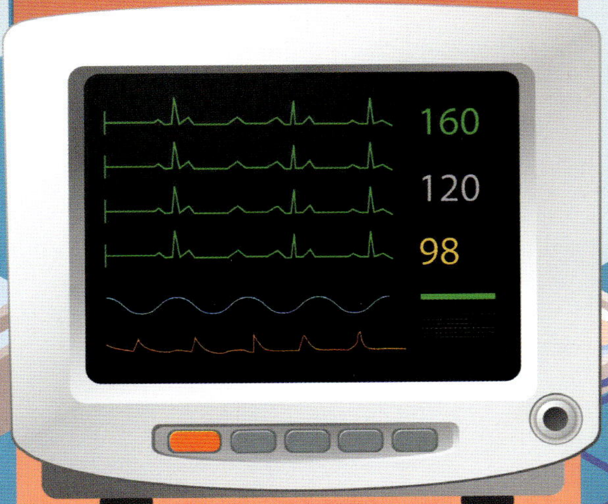

Life support

Patients in intensive care usually require some form of life support. They may need a ventilator to help them breathe, or a tube inserted to provide fluids, nutrition and medication. They may also be fitted with a catheter to remove urine from the bladder.

What happens in an operating theatre?

The operating theatre is where surgical operations are carried out. These might include mending bones, muscles and tendons, amputating or reattaching limbs, or removing, transplanting or repairing organs. The surgeon is in overall charge of an operation alongside a team of other specialists. These include a surgeon's assistant; an anaesthetist, who keeps the patient unconscious and/or pain free during the operation; and a theatre nurse, who prepares the patient, hands equipment and materials to the surgeon as required, and acts as a link between the surgical team and the rest of the hospital.

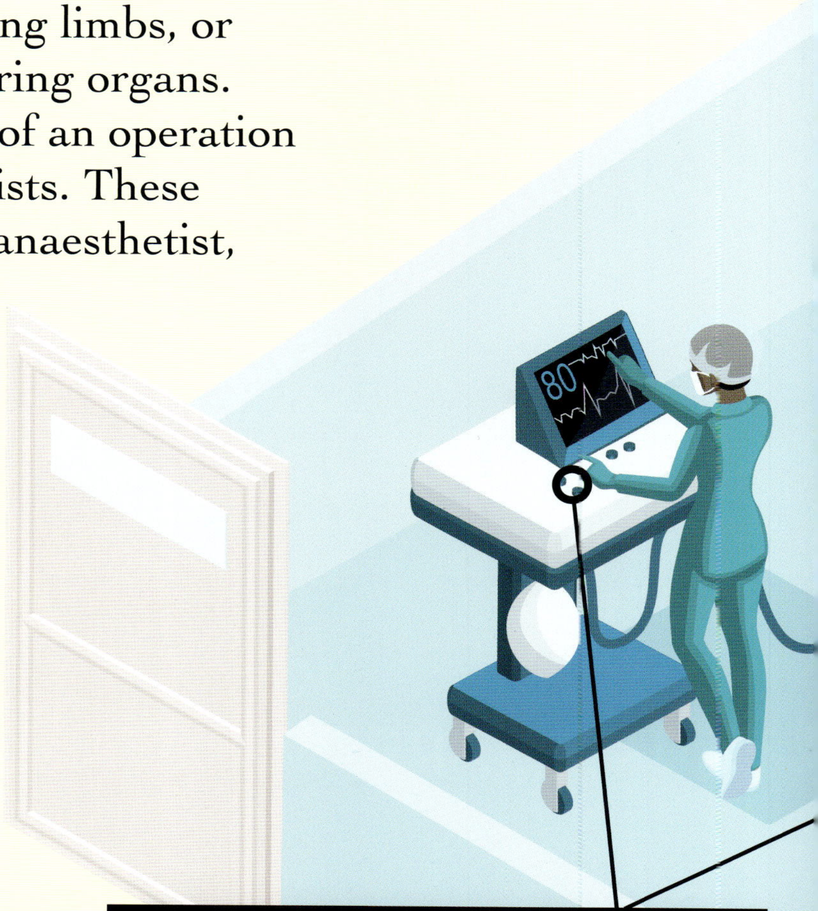

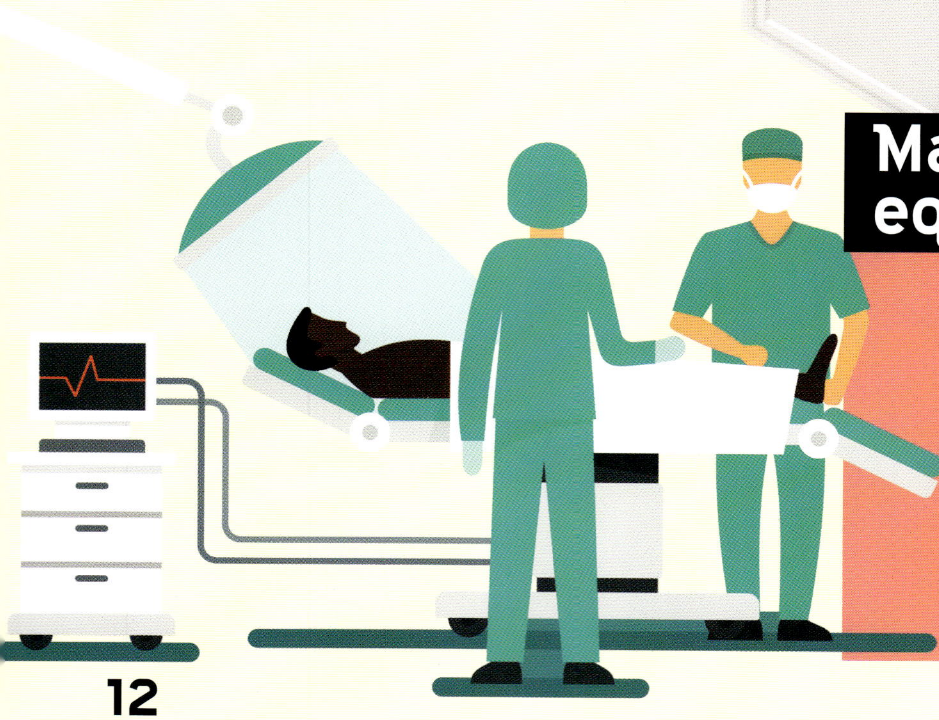

Machines and equipment

The operating table can be raised, lowered and tilted in different directions. Sterile (germ-free) surgical instruments are laid out for use. A monitor records the patient's vital signs. The anaesthesia machine administers a mixture of gases to the patient.

The rooms

Operating theatres are spacious and well-lit with easy-to-clean surfaces. Great efforts are made to keep them germ-free. Their temperature and humidity is controlled and machines filter dust and other particles from the air. They have a back-up electricity supply in case of power cuts.

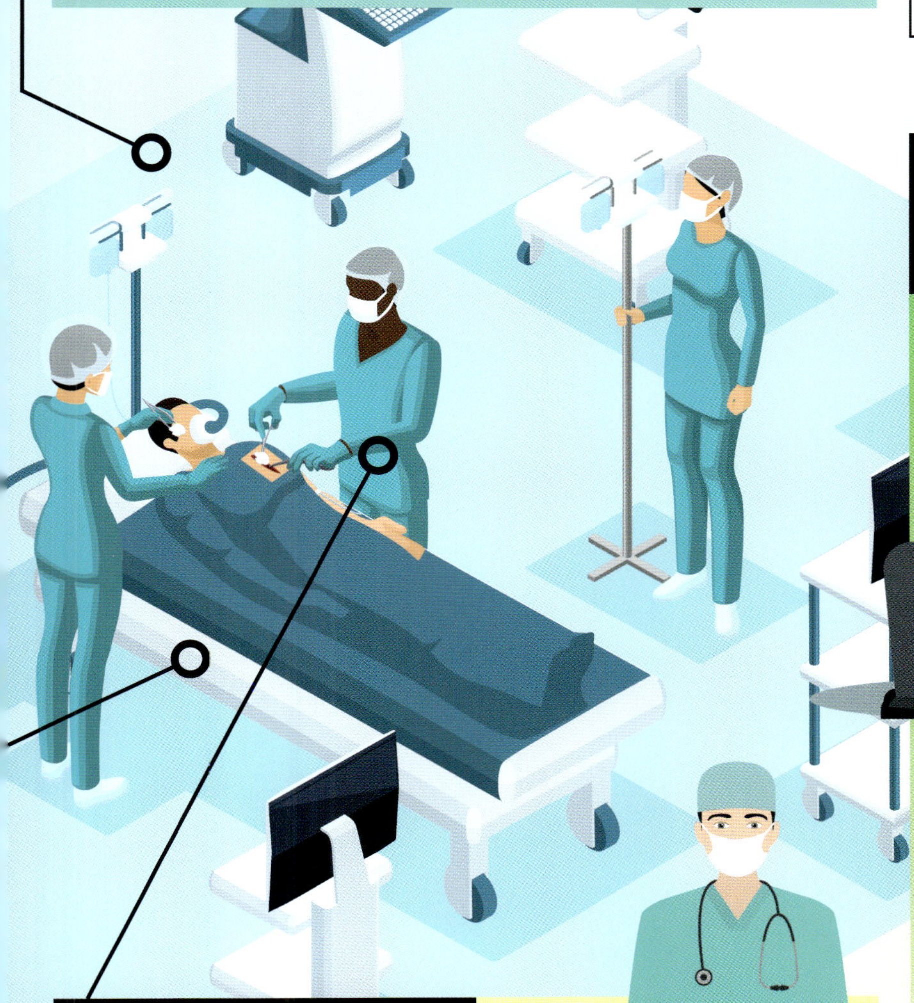

You are here

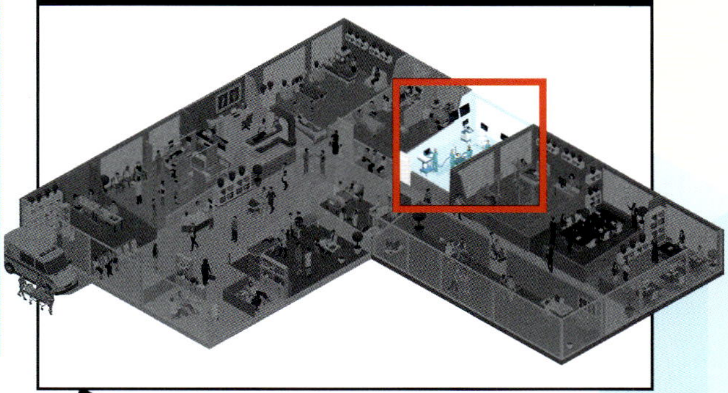

S.T.E.A.M solutions

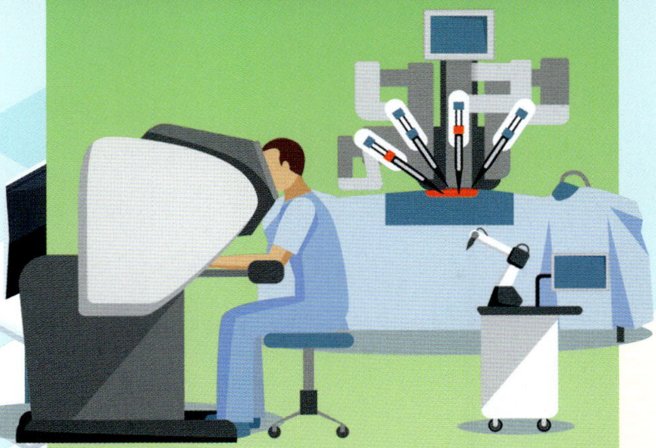

Robotic surgery is carried out around the world. A surgeon sitting at a console watching a magnified, 3-D view of the operation can direct the robot's movements using two joysticks. Robots have many advantages: they do not get tired or suffer from tremors, and they can make very small, precise movements. They are not limited by the size of the human hand and can manipulate tiny tools in very small spaces inside the body.

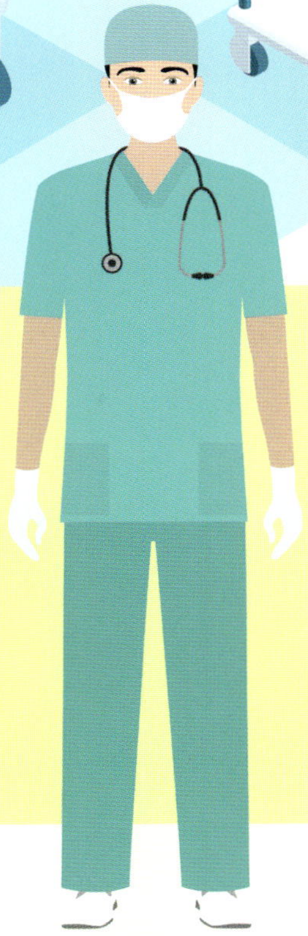

Clothing

The surgical team wear special clothing to prevent the spread of germs. They wear a cap over their hair, masks over their mouth and nose, disposable latex gloves, long gowns and protective covers on their shoes.

Can hospitals provide scans of the body?

It is possible to look inside a patient's body to diagnose what is wrong with them or to examine the progress of a disease. Specialist doctors called radiologists use a range of imaging techniques, the most well-known being X-rays. These rays pass through most of the human body, but not its bones or teeth, so these show up in X-ray photographs. X-rays do not show most of the body's soft tissues, muscles or organs, and they only show 2-D images, mostly in black-and-white. For more detailed images, radiologists must use other techniques.

Ultrasound

Ultrasound sends pulses of very high-pitched sound into the body. Sound waves that bounce back off the body's organs like echoes are picked up by detectors and a computer analyses these to form a picture. Ultrasound is the safest of all imaging techniques.

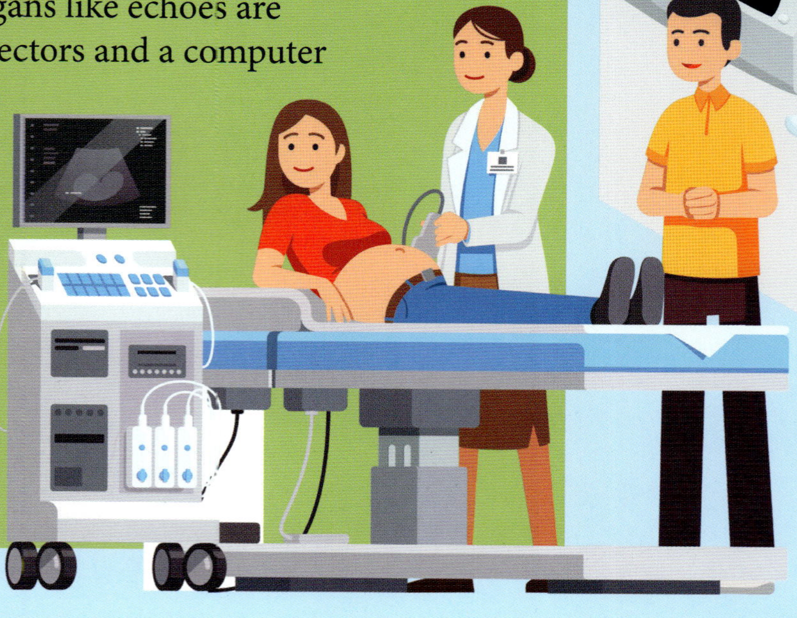

PET scans

The patient is given a drink, most commonly glucose, that has been tagged with a radioisotope (a radioactive version of an element such as oxygen). The radioisotope gives off signals inside the patient's body that are picked up by the scanner. PET scans can help diagnose cancer or brain damage.

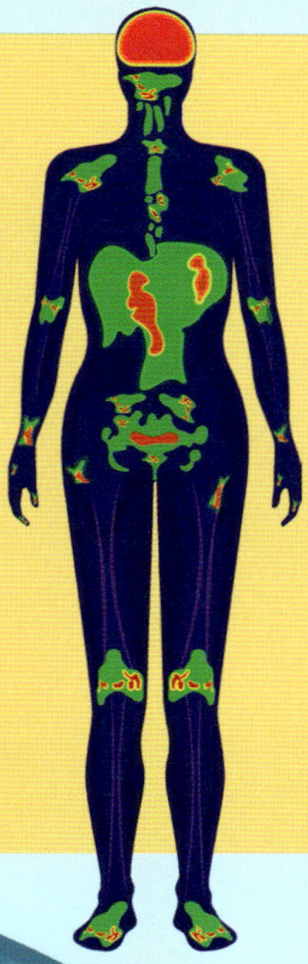

You are here

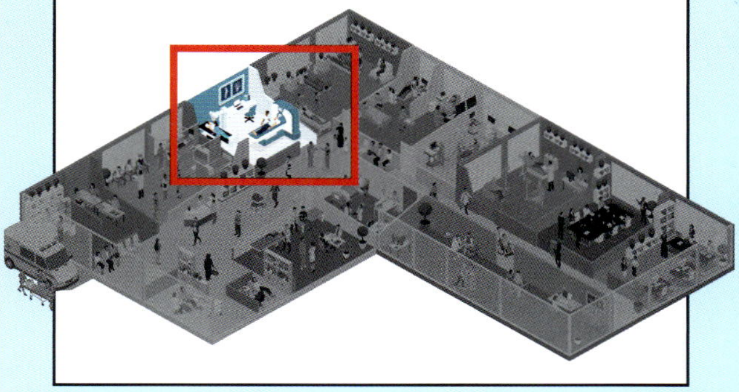

S.T.E.A.M solutions

Magnetic resonance imaging (MRI) is a scanning technique used to produce images of the body's soft tissues. It works by detecting hydrogen atoms in the body. MRI directs magnets and radio waves at the body, causing the body's hydrogen atoms to send out weak magnetic signals. The signals vary and a computer analyses these variations to create an image of the different organs and tissues within the body.

CT scans

Computed tomography (CT) scanners take X-ray photos of the body from different angles. A computer analyses this data to build up an image of a slice of the body, including its soft tissues.

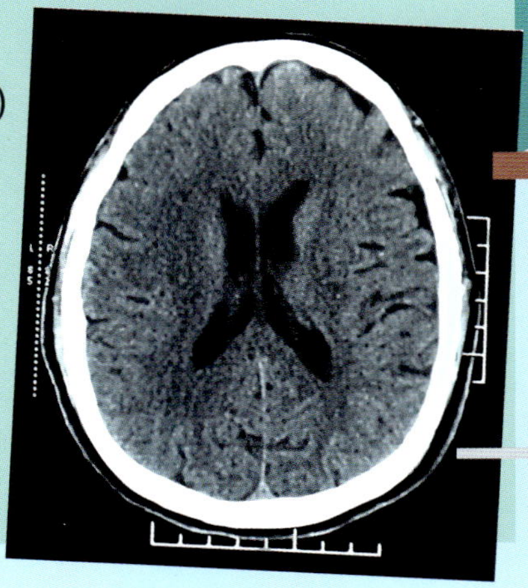

How are heart and blood problems treated?

Doctors in the cardiology ward treat diseases of the heart and blood vessels. They are called cardiologists. They advise patients on the risks of heart disease and how to prevent it. They diagnose heart problems by checking blood pressure, heartbeat, pulse and breathing. Sometimes they undertake further tests such as an X-ray, blood test or ECG (which tests the heart's rhythm and electrical activity). Cardiologists are not surgeons, but they might perform small procedures such as cardiac catheterisations – inserting a thin tube into a blood vessel to examine how well the heart is working.

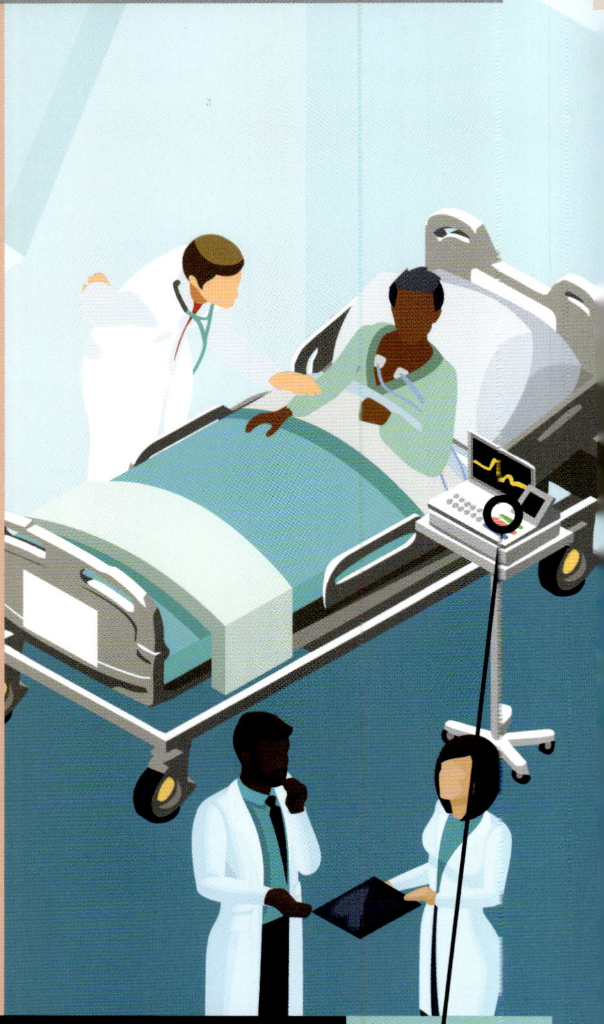

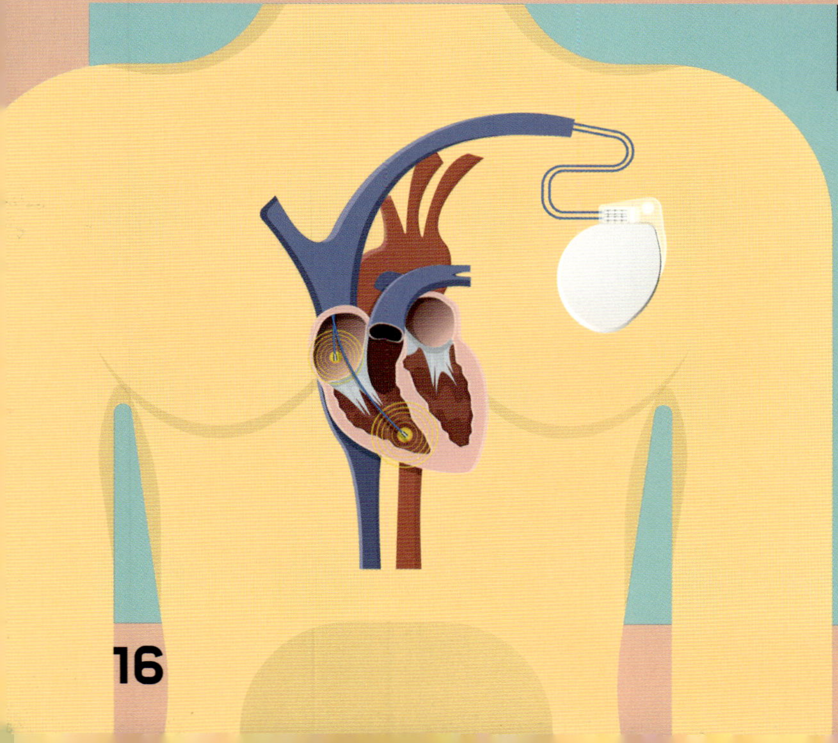

Heartbeat

Sometimes the heart can beat too fast or too slow. In serious cases this can cause lightheadedness, shortness of breath or chest pain. It can even lead to heart failure or cardiac arrest. Cardiologists may suggest certain medicines, or the implanting of a pacemaker, a device that sends out electrical impulses to regulate the patient's heartbeat.

Blood vessels

Cardiologists also deal with blood vessel disorders. Narrowed arteries are caused when fatty deposits called plaques form on artery walls. It can lead to high blood pressure and blood clots which can be life-threatening if a clot blocks a blood vessel.

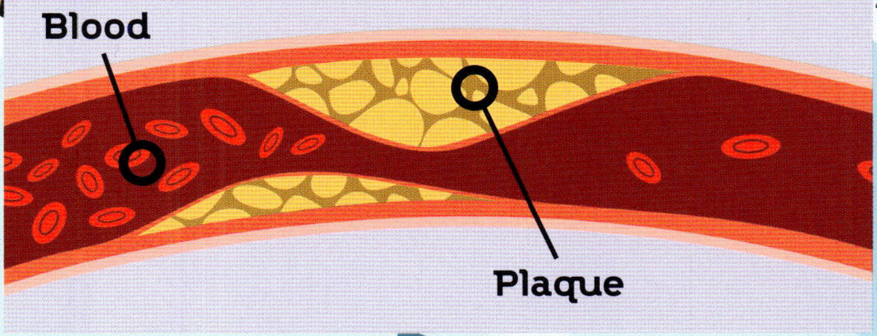

You are here

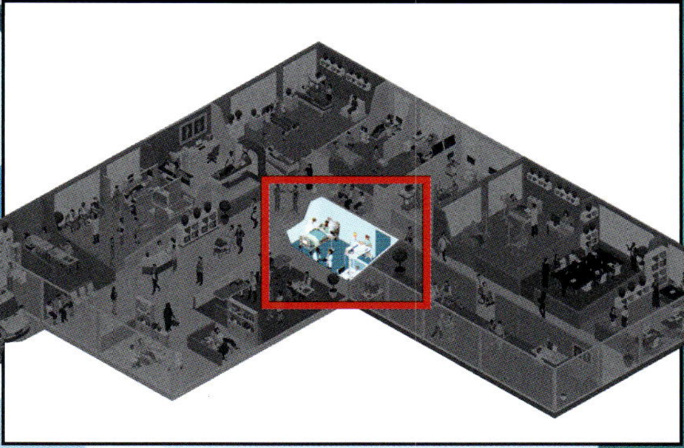

S.T.E.A.M solutions

An echocardiogram is used in the diagnosis of heart disease. It's a scan that gives a detailed view of the heart. A probe emits high-pitched sound waves that are reflected off the internal structures of the heart. Detectors pick up the echoes and translate them into real-time images on a screen. Echocardiograms can reveal the size and shape of the heart and can be used to investigate heart arrhythmia and heart attacks.

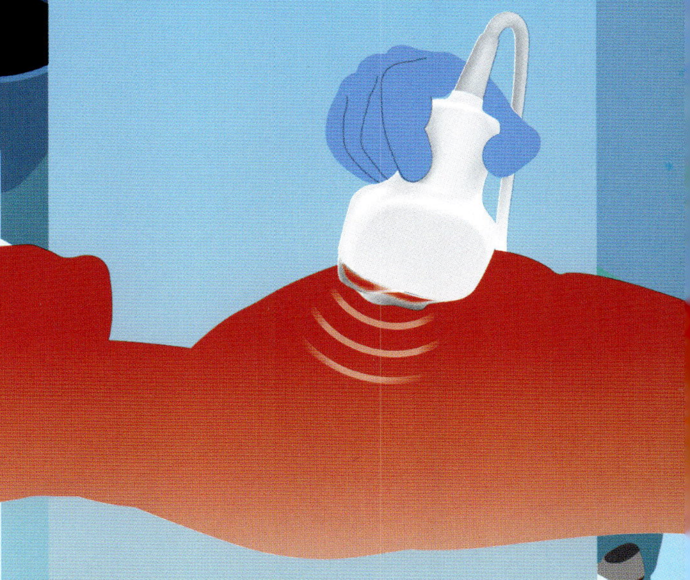

Blood problems

The haematology ward treats common blood problems like haemophilia, when blood does not clot properly; anaemia, when the blood can't transport enough oxygen; and leukaemia, which is when people have too many white blood cells in their blood.

How are problems of digestion treated?

Human digestion is a complex process. Patients with digestive problems are treated by gastroenterologists, doctors who specialise in disorders of the stomach, intestines, liver, gallbladder and pancreas. Conditions they must deal with include gastrointestinal bleeding, inflammatory bowel disease, jaundice and gastroenteritis.

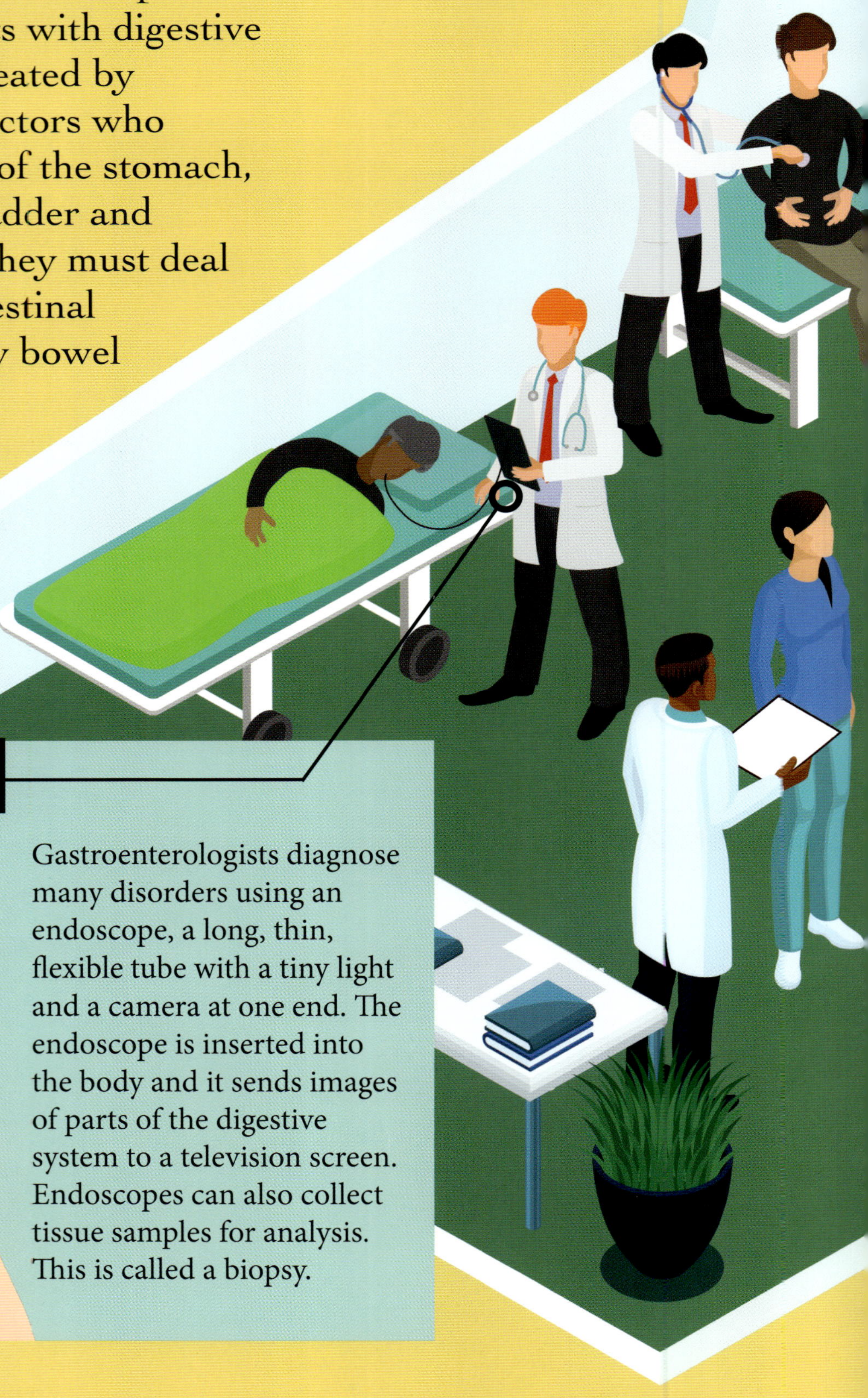

Endoscopy

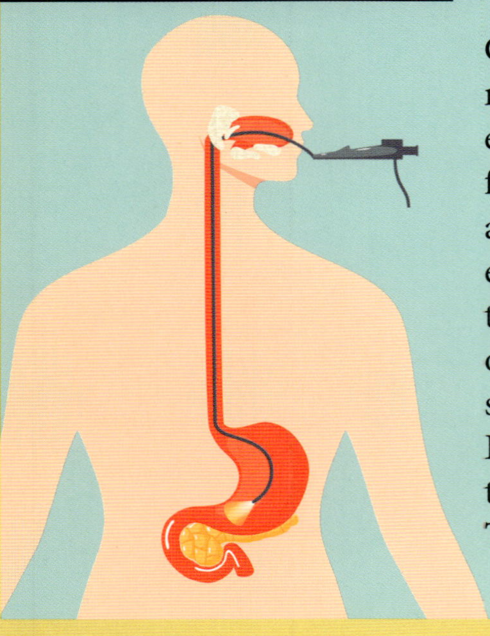

Gastroenterologists diagnose many disorders using an endoscope, a long, thin, flexible tube with a tiny light and a camera at one end. The endoscope is inserted into the body and it sends images of parts of the digestive system to a television screen. Endoscopes can also collect tissue samples for analysis. This is called a biopsy.

Internal surgery

Endoscopes with surgical instruments attached to them can be used to carry out repairs to the digestive system without invasive surgery. They can remove kidney stones, treat a bleeding stomach ulcer or remove small tumours.

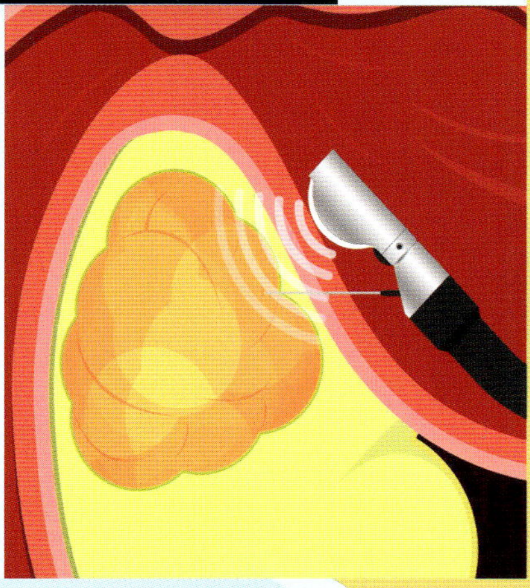

You are here

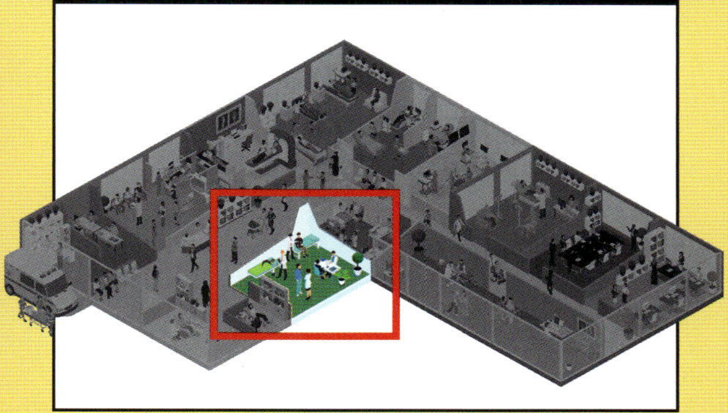

S.T.E.A.M solutions

The narrow tubes of the small intestine are not easily reached by an endoscope. Patients are often given a capsule endoscopy, a tiny wireless camera inside a pill-sized capsule that the patient swallows. The capsule travels through the small intestine, taking thousands of photographs that are transmitted to a recorder the patient wears on a belt around their waist.

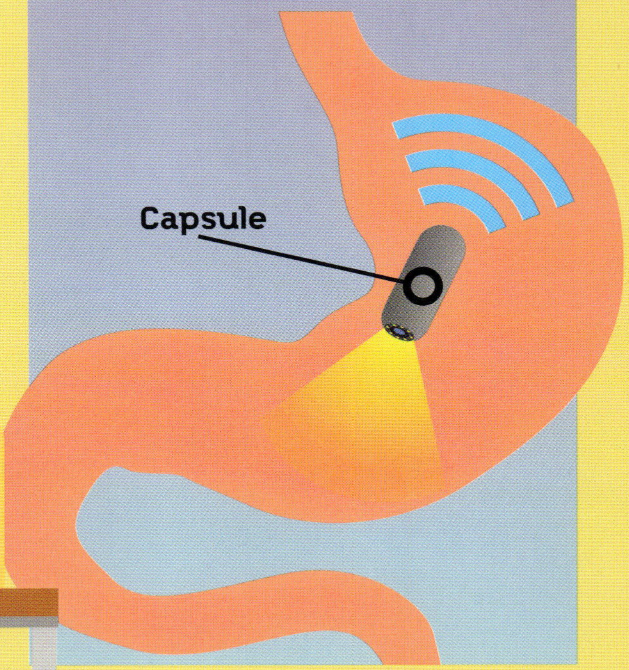

Aftercare

After treatment the patient will usually be advised on how to improve their diet and lifestyle. Some hospitals run a dedicated telephone help line.

How do hospitals help with childbirth?

Hospitals play a role at all stages of childbirth. Women make regular visits to hospital for screening tests throughout their pregnancy. Most babies are born in the maternity ward of a hospital where women have access to a midwife and, if necessary, an obstetrician (a doctor specialising in childbirth) and anaesthetists to help with pain. If any baby has a problem, it is taken to the hospital's neonatal (baby care) unit.

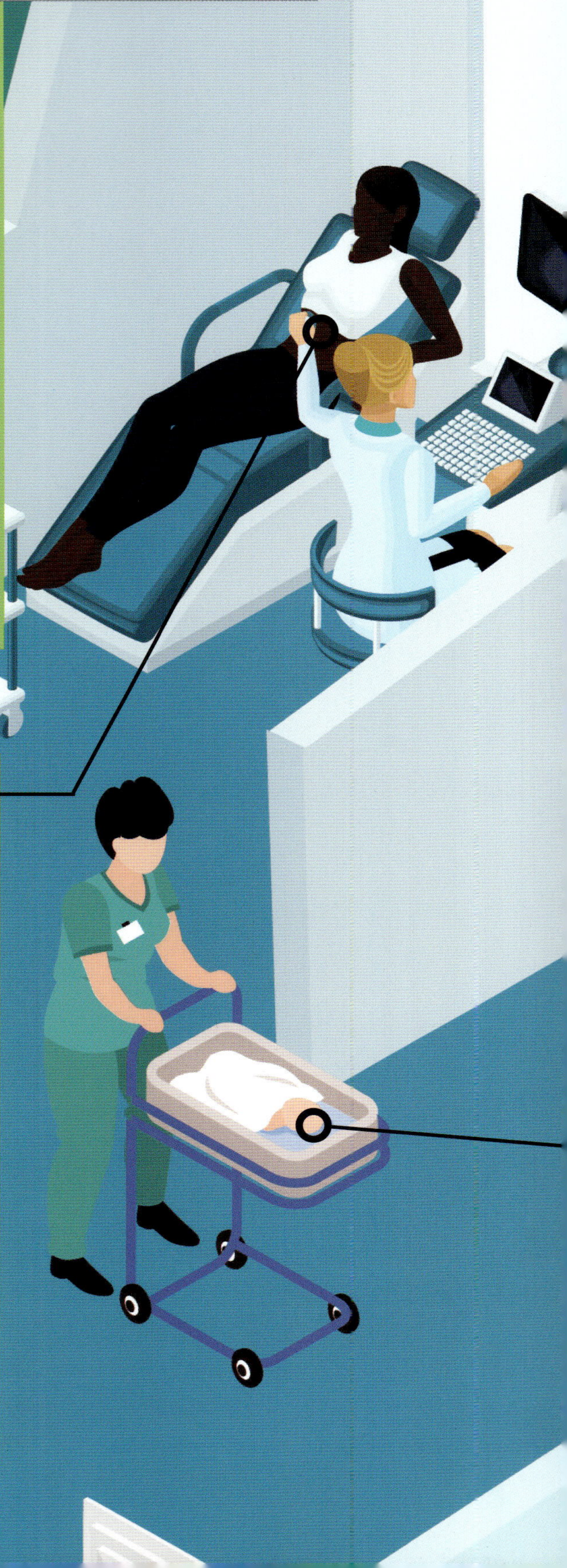

During pregnancy

Ultrasound scans monitor foetal development and can detect physical abnormalities. Blood tests can show whether the mother has any inherited disorders or infections that she could pass on to her child.

Labour and childbirth

During childbirth some women choose to have an epidural (an anaesthetic that numbs them from the waist down). The midwife is there to assist during the birth and afterwards.

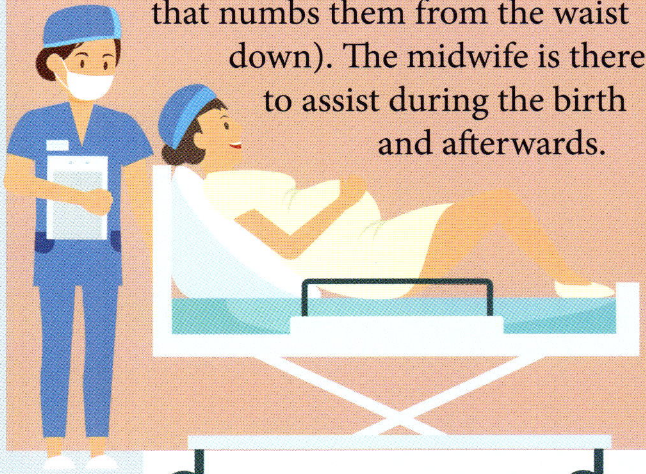

You are here

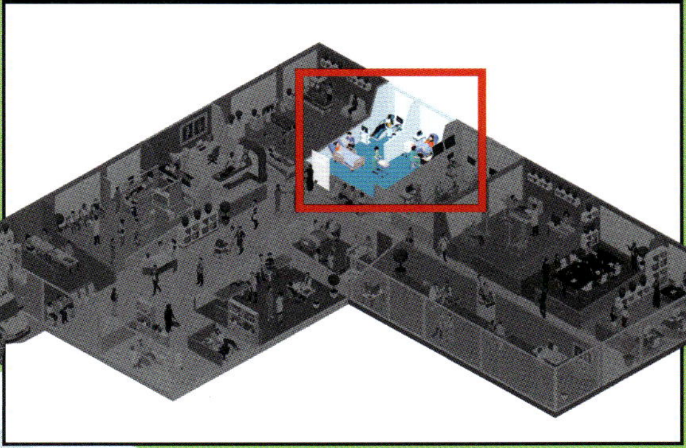

S.T.E.A.M solutions

Newborn babies who are sick or premature are extremely vulnerable. They are kept in an incubator, which provides an isolated, carefully regulated environment that protects them from infection, cold, noise and drafts. Incubators contain various items including a blood pressure monitor, an oxygen hood or ventilator for infants that need help with breathing.

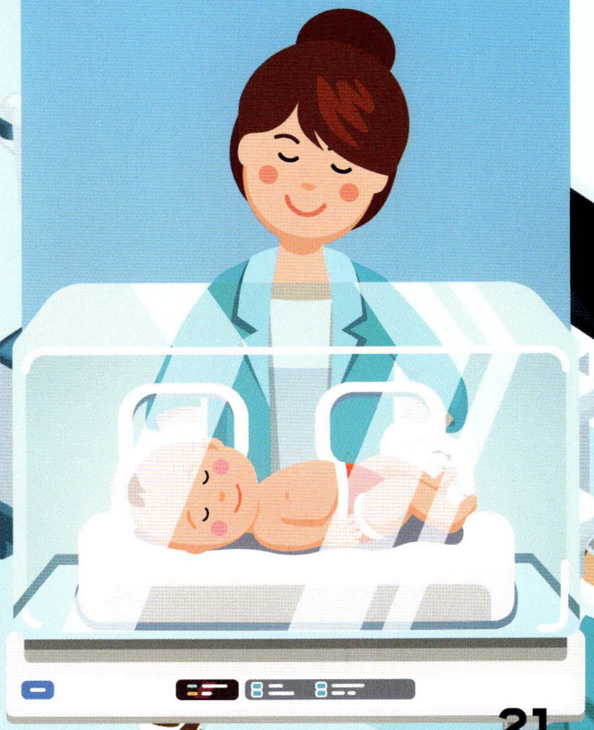

Neonatal care

Newborn babies that are sick, have a low birth weight or are premature (less than 37 weeks' gestation) are taken to the hospital's neonatal unit. Here, staff can monitor their breathing and heart rate, give them more oxygen, treat low body temperature or blood sugar, and help them feed.

Where are cancer patients treated?

Cancer is a disease caused by the uncontrolled division of cells that can result in a dangerous growth called a tumour. Cancer patients are treated in an oncology ward. An oncologist (cancer doctor) must first diagnose the cancer using medical imaging, biopsies and endoscopies. Once the cancer is diagnosed, the oncologist talks through treatment options with the patient. A patient's treatment plan usually uses a combination of therapies.

Stem cell

Some cancers stop stem cells from developing normally in a patient's bone marrow, which then creates abnormal blood cells. A stem cell transplant gives a patient new stem cells. The stem cells are collected from the patient, the patient receives chemotherapy, then the stem cells are put back in their blood. Patients may also receive donor stem cells.

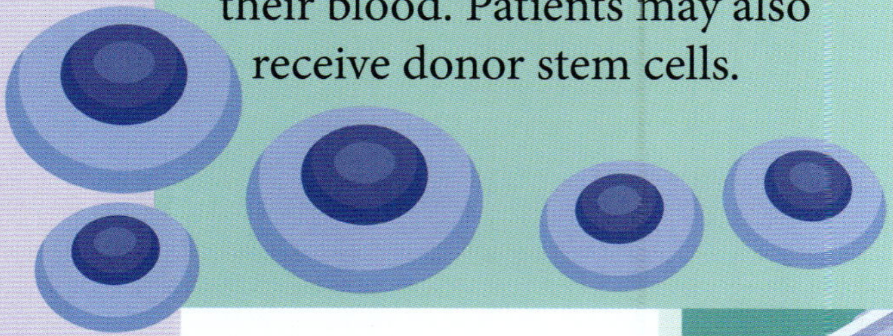

Chemotherapy

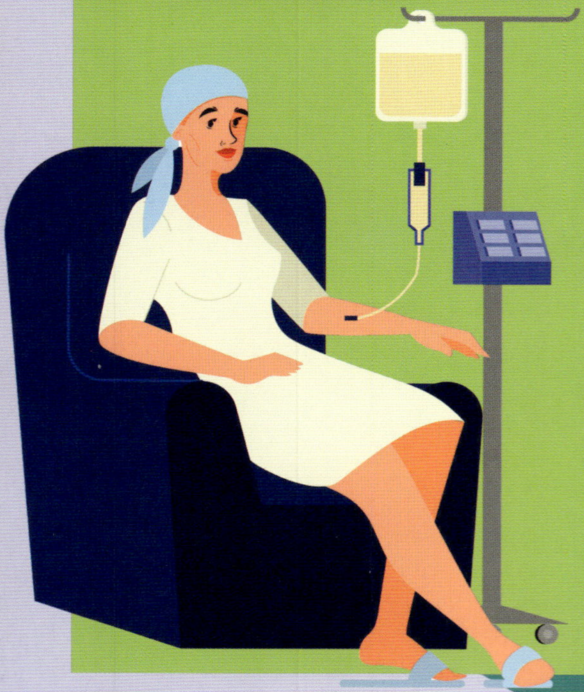

Drugs can help to shrink tumours. Chemotherapy works on 'active' cells (cells that are growing and dividing). These include cancer cells and healthy cells. It has many side-effects, such as headaches, muscle pain, mouth sores, digestive problems and hair loss.

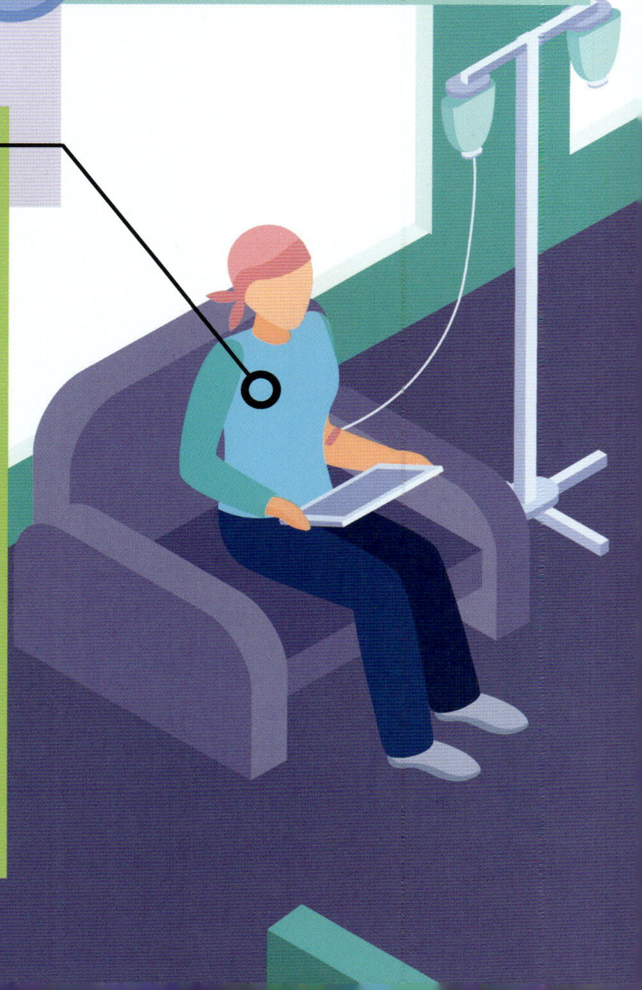

Immunotherapy

Immunotherapy uses natural proteins called antibodies to improve the patient's immune system, so that it can fight the cancer. Monoclonal antibodies, made in a laboratory, can be used to attack cancer cells directly. Alternatively, they can tag the cancer cells so the immune system can find and destroy them.

You are here

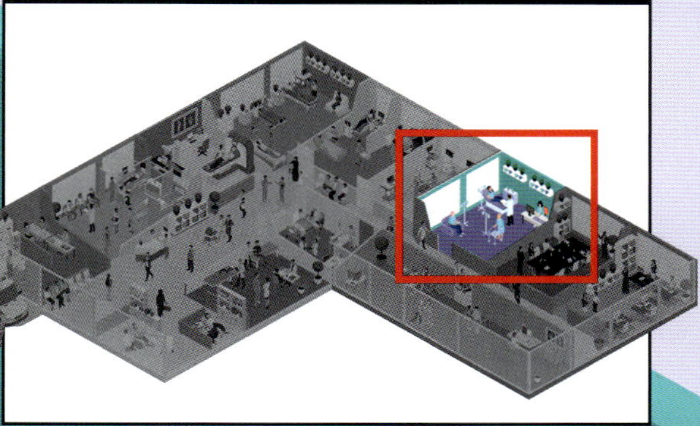

S.T.E.A.M solutions

Radiation therapy uses high-energy X-rays or protons to shrink or destroy cancer cells, or to slow tumour growth. External-beam radiation therapy is the most common kind. A machine called a linear accelerator directs a beam of radiation at the tumour. Computer software adjusts the beam's size and shape to avoid targeting healthy tissue.

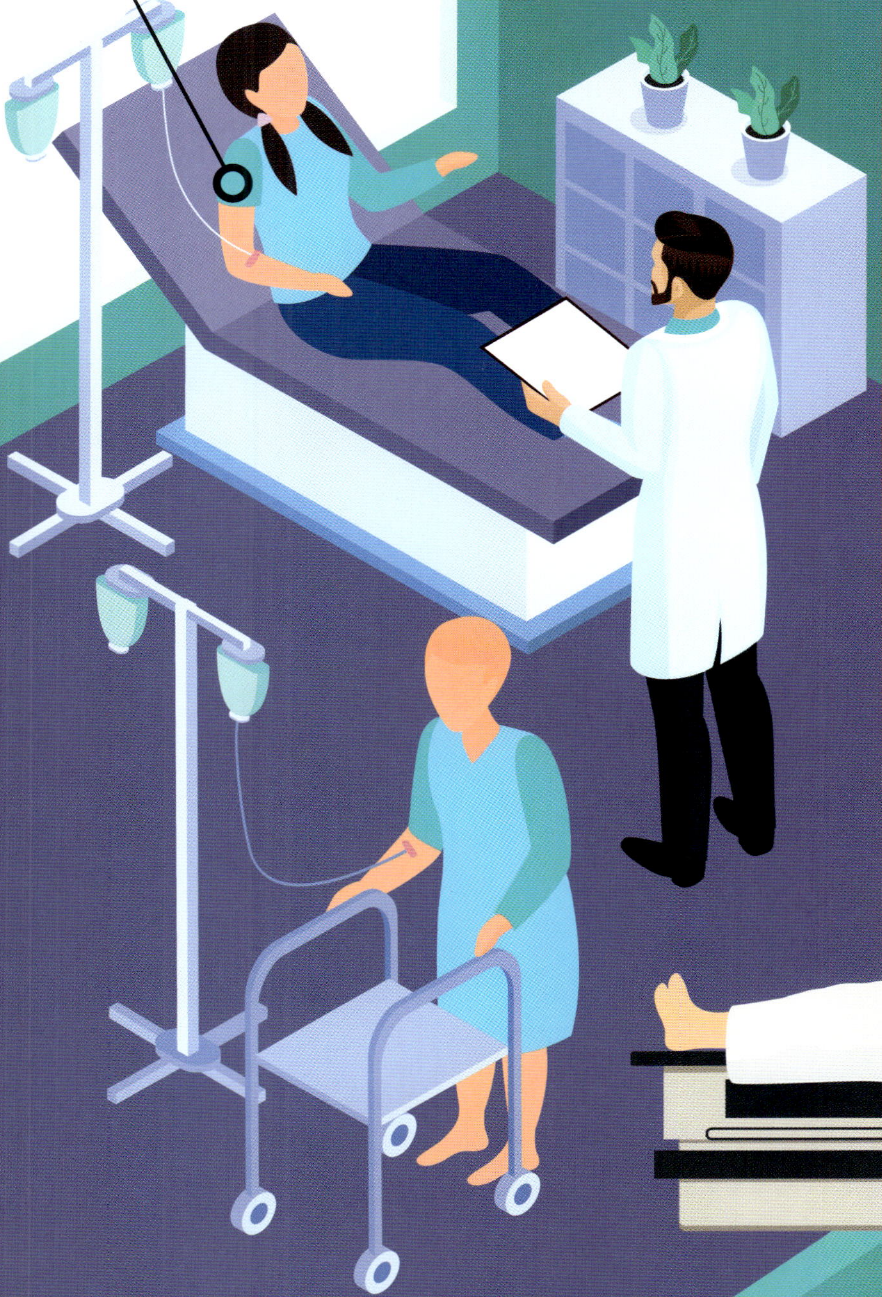

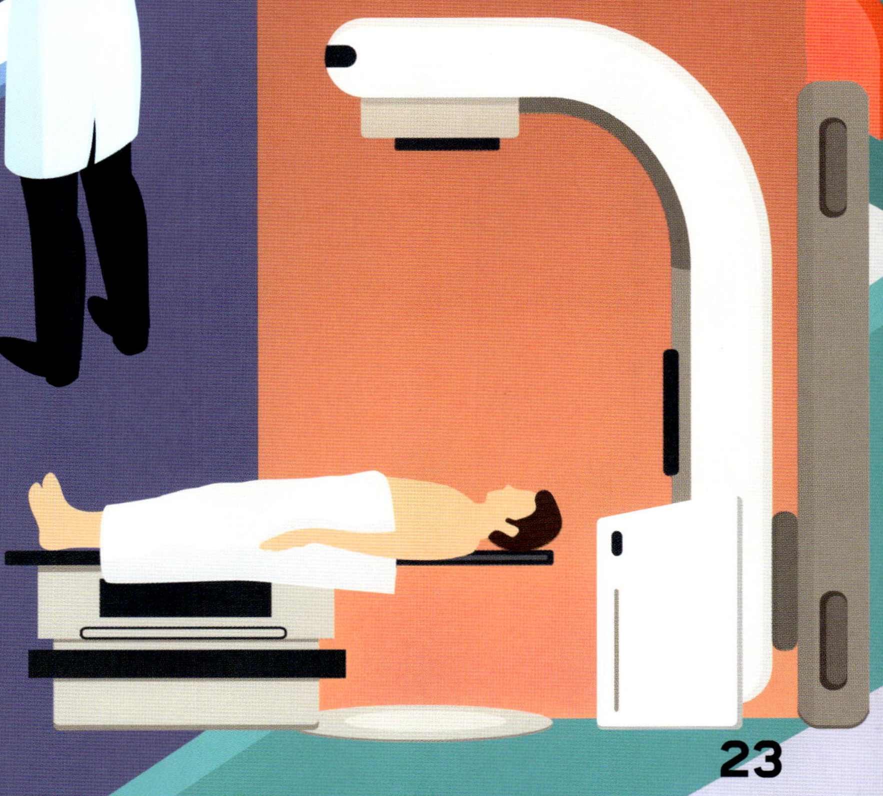

Mending fractures

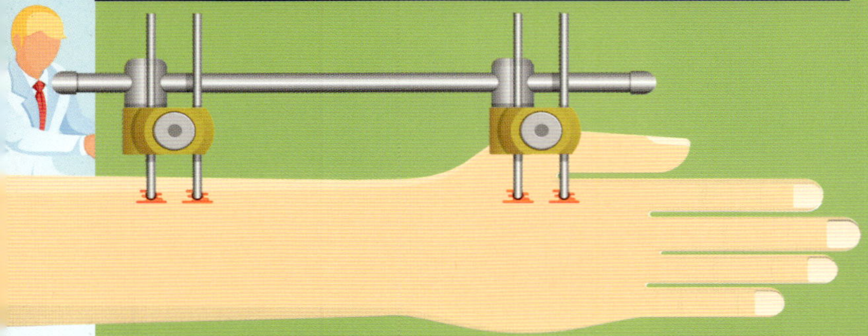

Different methods are used to mend broken bones. One method is to hold the broken pieces of bone in position with metal plates, pins or screws while the bone is healing. These can be temporary or permanent. If the bone is shattered or irreparable, they may take a bone sample from the patient's body to replace the damaged section. This is called a bone graft.

Soft tissue repair

Orthopaedic surgeons often carry out repairs to muscles, tendons and ligaments. If a person loses the nerves in a muscle, a tendon transfer can utilise the power of a working muscle (with nerves) to restore the weakened muscle function.

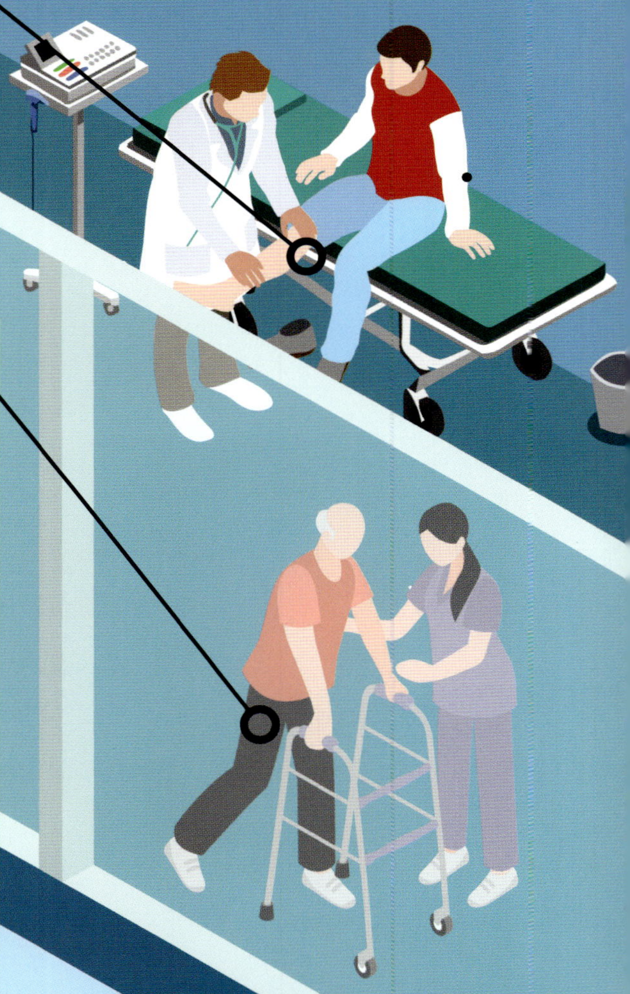

Joint replacement

If a patient's joint becomes diseased or damaged, orthopaedic surgeons can replace it with a metal, plastic or ceramic device called a prosthesis. It is designed to replicate the movement of a normal, healthy joint.

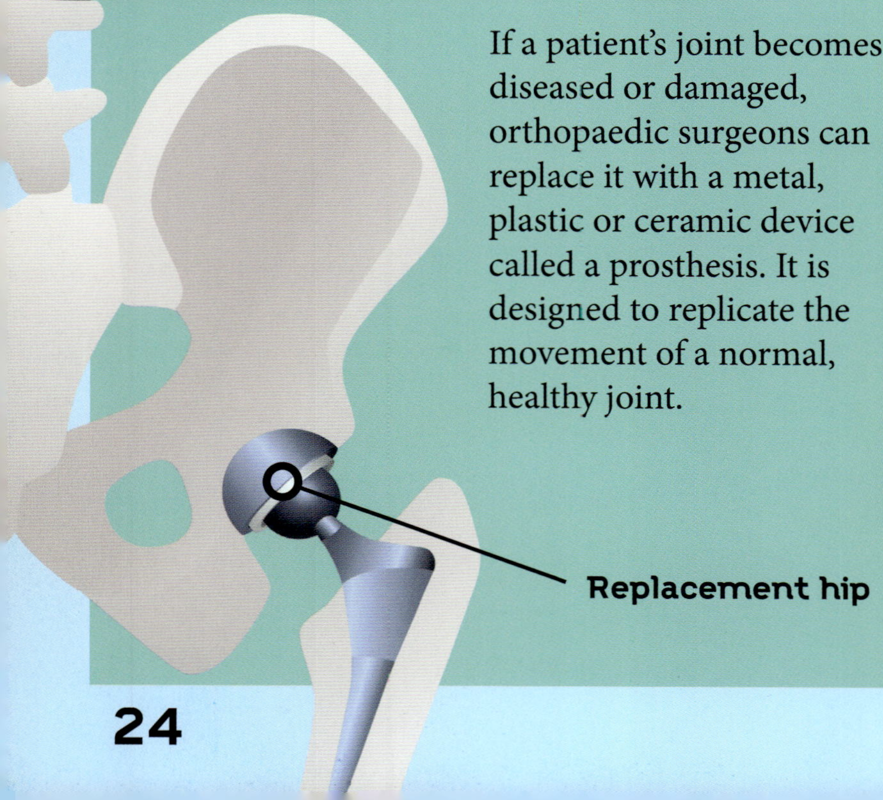

Where are muscles and bones treated?

Patients with muscle, bone or joint problems attend the orthopaedic ward which treats injuries, degenerative conditions, infections or tumours. Orthopaedic surgeons treat sports injuries, back pain, arthritis, club foot, bow legs and deformed spines. They mend fractures, lengthen limbs and replace joints. Some specialise in specific parts of the body, or choose particular fields such as paediatrics (treating children), trauma (accidents) or sports medicine.

You are here

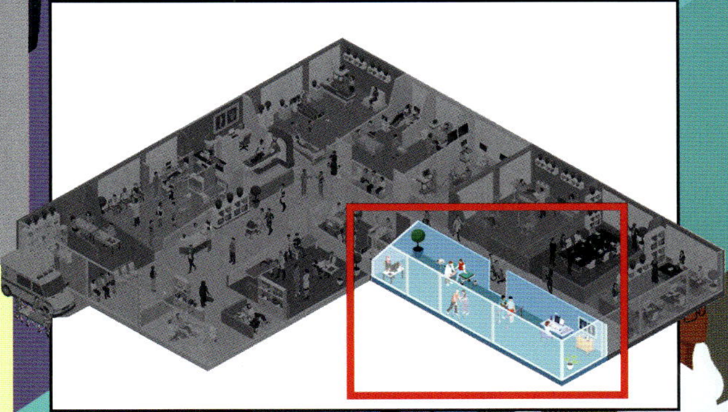

S.T.E.A.M solutions

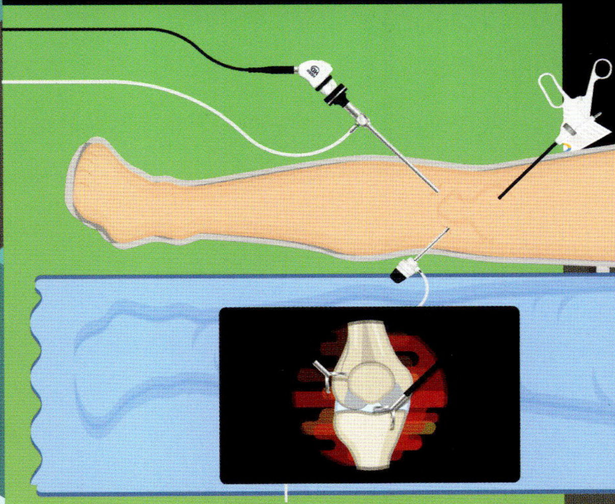

When operating on a joint, surgeons often use a procedure called an arthroscopy. The equipment used is miniature, so it needs only small incisions. An arthroscope, fitted with a tiny lens and light, is inserted into the joint. The images are sent through a fibre optic cable to a screen. The surgeons then make repairs by inserting specially designed surgical instruments through the incision site. Arthroscopy makes patient recovery time much quicker.

What other medical treatments are there?

Hospitals must be able to deal with many different injuries, conditions and ailments. There may be wards specialising in problems of the skin (dermatology); the ears, nose and throat (otorhinolaryngology); the eyes (ophthalmology); the nerves (neurology); the urinary system (urology); the female reproductive system (gynaecology); and the mind (psychiatry). There may also be a paediatric ward for children, and a geriatric ward for the elderly.

Dermatology

Dermatologists diagnose, treat and advise on problems with the skin, nails and hair. Cryosurgery is used to freeze warts, skin cancers and lesions before removing them. Lasers or ultraviolet light is used to treat birth marks, acne, eczema and other skin disorders, and to remove tattoos.

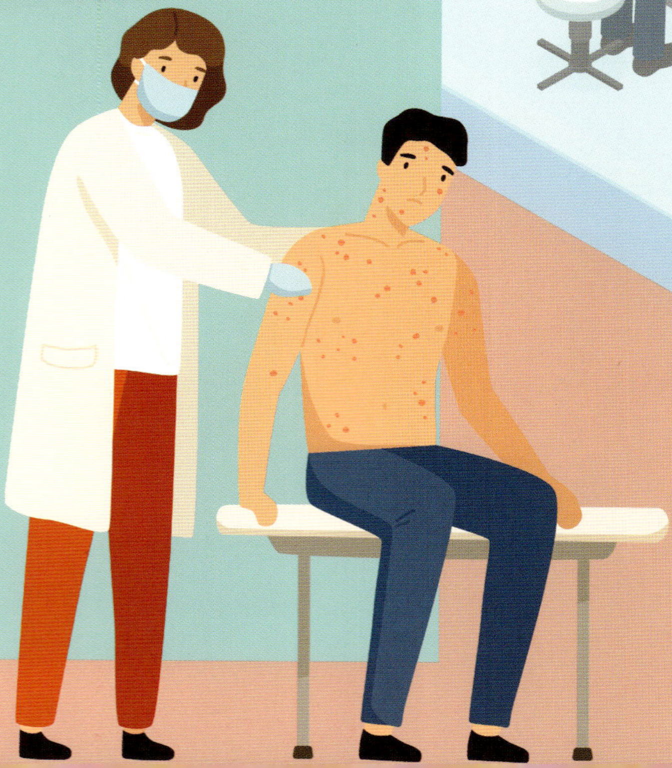

Ears, nose and throat

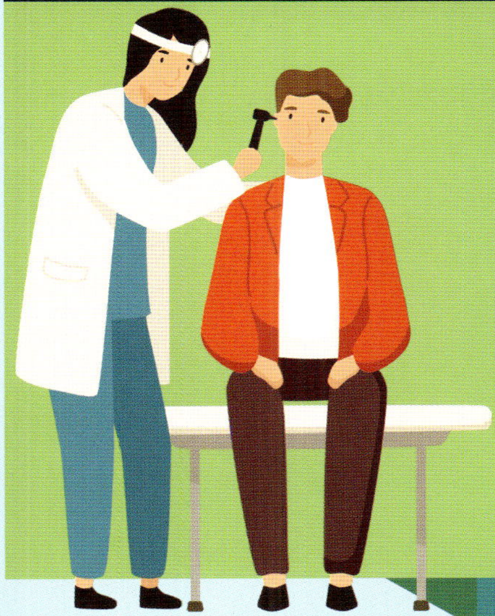

ENT surgeons treat injuries, diseases and infections to the ears, nose and throat, as well as problems with hearing, balance, smell, taste, voice, breathing and swallowing.

You are here

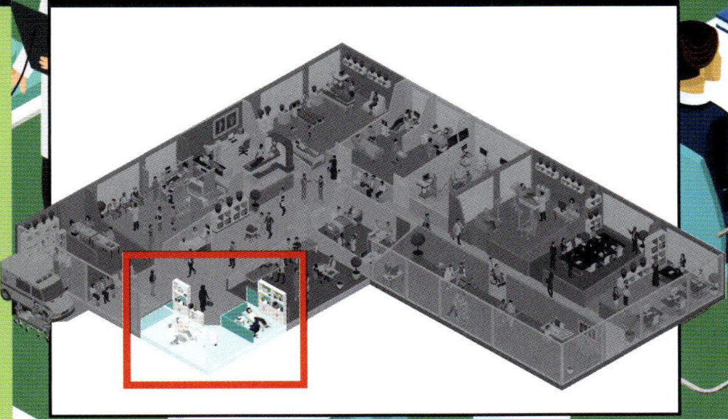

S.T.E.A.M solutions

Eye doctors use an instrument called an ophthalmoscope to examine the back of a patient's eye. This part of the eye, called the fundus, consists of the retina, optic disc and blood vessels. The doctor holds the instrument close to the patient's eye and shines a light through the pupil, which is transparent. The light is reflected off the fundus and the ophthalmoscope lens magnifies the view by up to fifteen times.

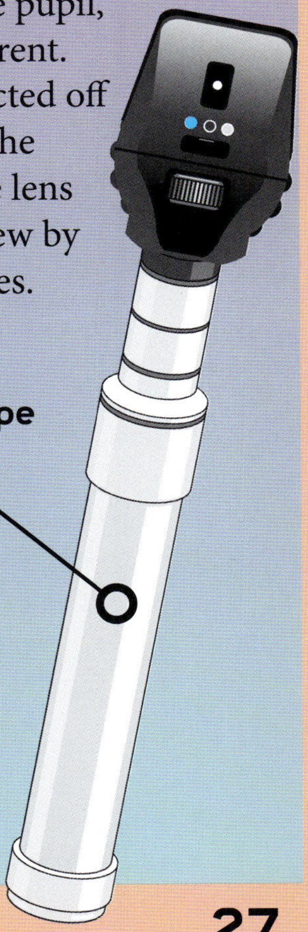

Psychiatry

Patients suffering from mental disorders, who might endanger themselves or others, are often hospitalised. There they will be cared for by trained staff and have access to talking therapies and medication.

What other departments are there?

All hospital wards rely on the support of other departments. The radiology department provides medical imaging. Other support departments include the pharmacy, which stocks medicines; pathology, which studies blood and other specimens from patients; sterile services, which removes germs from medical equipment; and medical social workers, who provide counselling and practical assistance for patients with physical or mental illness.

Pharmacy

A hospital pharmacy supplies medicines for patients on the wards. Pharmacists work with doctors and nurses to ensure patients receive the safest, most appropriate and cost-effective medication for their needs.

Pathology

The pathology laboratory test blood and tissue samples for disease and investigate viral and bacterial infections. They locate compatible donor organs for transplant surgery, provide blood transfusions, and store and preserve stem cells.

You are here

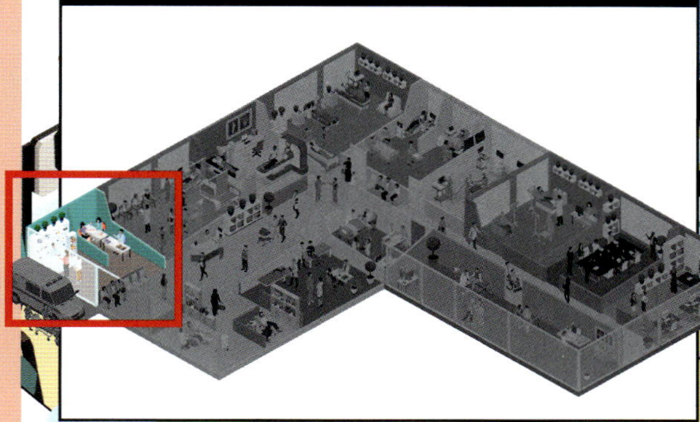

S.T.E.A.M solutions

Different methods are used to sterilise a hospital's medical equipment. With steam sterilisation, equipment is placed in a chamber called an autoclave, which is filled with high-temperature steam to kill all germs. Some medical tools, such as endoscopes, can be damaged by the high temperature and humidity of steam sterilisation. These are sterilised at low temperature using hydrogen peroxide plasma in a process called oxidation.

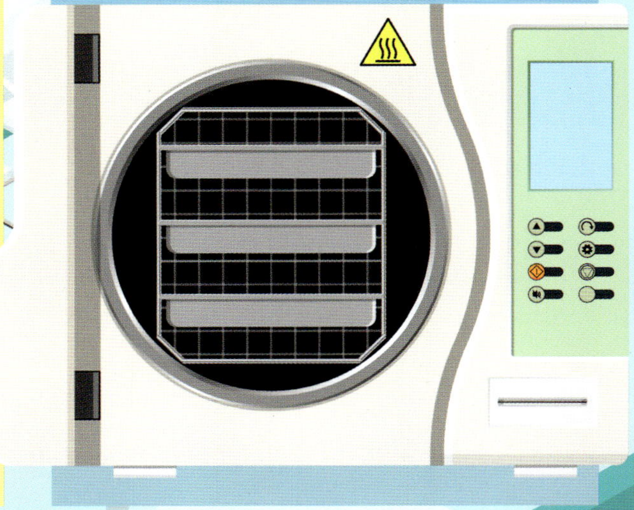

Medical social workers

Medical social workers might set up support groups for families with dying relatives, offer counselling for substance abusers, or help patients apply for government or community assistance.

Glossary

Administer Manage and be responsible for the running of (an organisation).

Arrhythmia A condition in which the heart beats with an irregular or abnormal rhythm.

Artery A blood vessel that carries blood from the heart to other parts of the body.

Bacterial infection A disease caused by tiny organisms called bacteria.

Biopsy An examination of tissue removed from the body to discover the presence, cause or extent of a disease.

Blood clot A mass of semi-solid blood.

Blood pressure The pressure of blood in the circulatory system. This tells doctors, for example, about the force of the heart beat and the elasticity of the arteries' walls.

Blood transfusion The injection of blood taken from a healthy person into a patient.

Budget An estimate of income and expenditure for a set period of time.

Cardiac arrest A sudden stopping of the heart.

Diagnosis The identification of an illness by examining its symptoms.

Eczema A medical condition in which patches of skin become inflamed with blisters that cause itching and bleeding.

Endoscopy A procedure in which a device is introduced into the body to give a view of its interior.

Foetal Relating to a foetus, an unborn human more than eight weeks after conception.

Gallbladder A small organ beneath the liver in which bile is stored after secretion by the liver and before release into the intestine.

Gastroenteritis Inflammation of the stomach and intestines causing vomiting and diarrhoea.

Humidity Moisture or dampness.

Incision A surgical cut made in flesh.

Jaundice A medical condition that results in a yellowing of the skin or the whites of the eyes.

Lesion Part of an organ or tissue that has suffered damage, such as a wound.

Ligament A band of tough, flexible tissue that connects two bones or holds together a joint.

Midwife A person trained to assist women in childbirth.

Pancreas An organ behind the stomach that secretes substances into the small intestine to help the process of digestion.

Paramedic A person trained to give emergency medical care to people who are seriously injured or ill to stabilise them before they are taken to hospital.

Radio waves A type of electromagnetic wave used in long-distance communication as well as MRI scanners.

Sedative A drug given to calm a patient or send them to sleep.

Sensor A device that detects or measures activity.

Stem cell An unspecialised cell that can develop into specialised cells, such as blood cells, skin cells or liver cells.

Sterilise Make something free of germs.

Tendon A flexible cord of tissue attaching a muscle to a bone.

Tissue The material of which animals and plants are made.

Tumour A swelling of part of the body caused by an abnormal growth of tissue.

Transplant Take living tissue or an organ and implant it in another body.

Ulcer An open sore on an internal or external surface of the body caused by a break in the skin or membrane.

Ultraviolet light A type of electromagnetic radiation with a wavelength shorter than that of violet but longer than that of X-rays.

Viral infection A disease caused by a microscopic parasite called a virus.

Vital signs Measurements that indicate the state of a patient's essential body functions. They are pulse rate, temperature, breathing rate and blood pressure.

Ward A hospital department.

X-ray An electromagnetic wave of high energy and very short wavelength, which is able to pass through many solid materials including the human body's organs and tissues, revealing the bones.

Index

LOOK & LEARN™

How A Hospital Works

Alex Woolf

Published in Great Britain in MMXXI by
Book House, an imprint of
The Salariya Book Company Ltd
25 Marlborough Place, Brighton BN1 1UB
www.salariya.com

ISBN: 978-1-913337-22-3

SALARIYA
SCRIBO BOOK HOUSE SCRIBBLERS

1 3 5 7 9 8 6 4 2

A CIP catalogue record for this book is available from the British Library.

Printed and bound in China.

Visit
www.salariya.com
for our online catalogue and
free fun stuff.

PAPER FROM SUSTAINABLE FORESTS

Author: Alex Woolf studied history at Essex University in England. He is the author of many books for children on science topics, including previous titles in the *You Wouldn't Want To Live Without* and *Science Of* series.

Editor: Nick Pierce

Artwork credits:
Rvector, Prokopeva Irina, Kddss, Macrovector, Golden Sikorka, Reenya, aurielaki, Igor Nazarenko, Andrew Rybalko, GoodStudio, metamorworks, rumruay, Graf Vishenka, Inspiring, jagoda, Iconic Bestiary, Irina Strelnikova, marina_ua, Teguh Jati Prasetyo, nfievet, Dmitry Kovalchuk, VectorPot /Shutterstock.com